D0568917

To Silas and Loudon, my very own Bob and Joss
—P.M.

To my dear friend Rui: in remembrance of our urban hikes together
—V.V.

Bob and Joss Take a Hike!
Text copyright © 2018 by Peter McCleery
Illustrations copyright © 2018 by Vin Vogel
All rights reserved. Manufactured in China.
No part of this book may be used or reproduced in any manner whatsoever without written permission except in the case
of brief quotations embodied in critical articles and reviews. For information address HarperCollins Children's Books, a
division of HarperCollins Publishers, 195 Broadway, New York, NY 10007.
www.harpercollinschildrens.com

ISBN 978-0-06-241532-5

The artist used Adobe Photoshop to create the digital illustrations for this book.
Design by Chelsea C. Donaldson
17 18 19 20 21 SCP   10 9 8 7 6 5 4 3 2 1
❖
First Edition

BOB and JOSS
Take a Hike!

by Peter McCleery • illustrated by Vin Vogel

HARPER
An Imprint of HarperCollinsPublishers

"Camping is boring," said Bob. "Let's do something."

"Let's take a hike," said Joss.

"Okay," said Bob. "But whatever you do, *don't forget the map.*"

"I won't forget the map," said Joss.

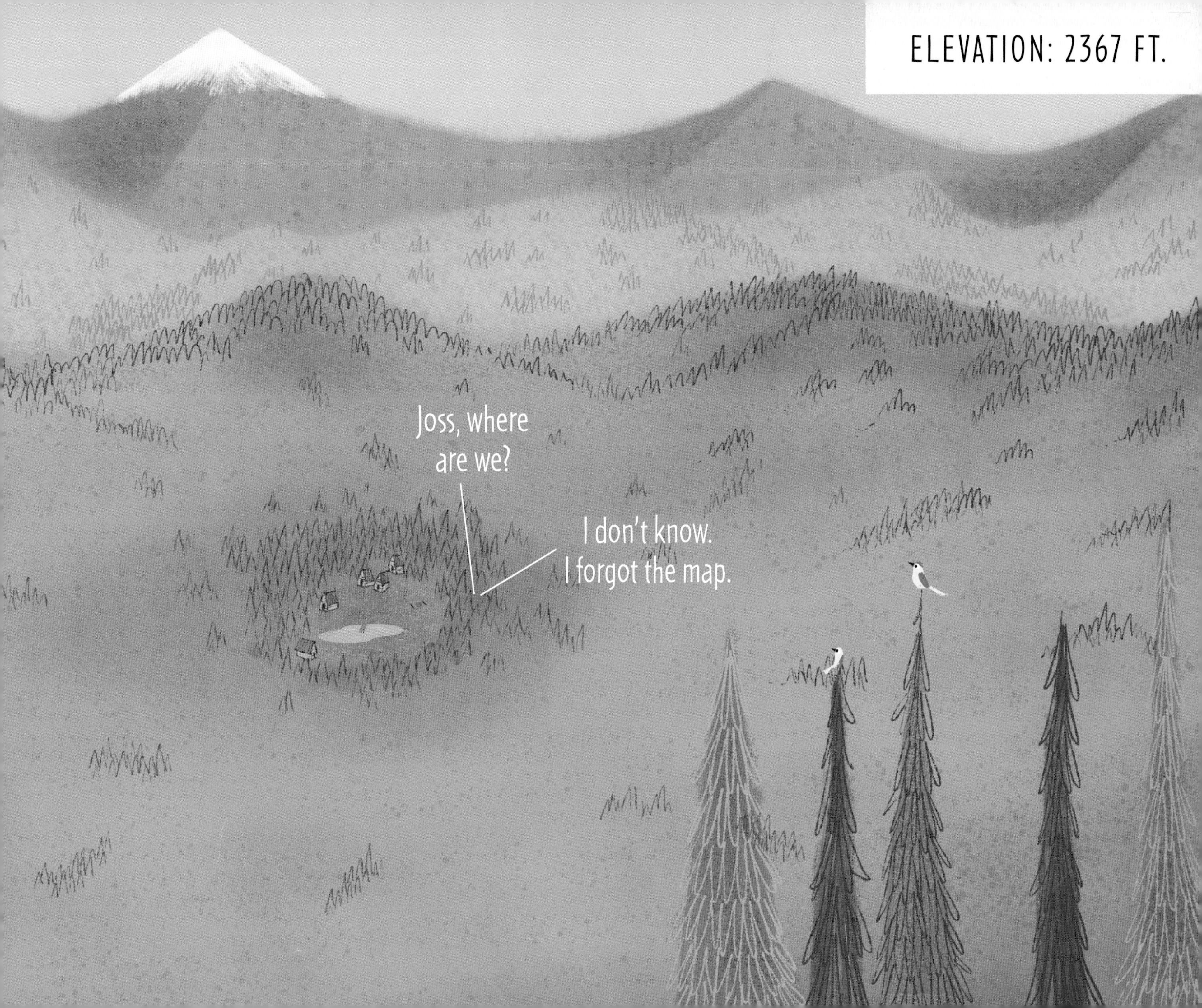
ELEVATION: 2367 FT.
Joss, where are we?
I don't know. I forgot the map.

"Which trail do we choose?" asked Bob.

"The right one!" said Joss.

"But which is the right one?"

"The right one is the right one," said Joss.

"What if the right way is wrong?" worried Bob.

"We'll find out when we don't get there," replied Joss.

"Are we on the right trail?" asked Bob.

"Yes, but it's wrong," said Joss.

"Does any of this look familiar?" asked Bob.

"It sure does!" said Joss.

"Oh, good! What looks familiar?"

"That tree. It looks just like all the other trees we passed," said Joss. "Probably the same species."

BZZZ

ELEVATION: 1790 FT.

Bob and Joss ventured farther into the wilderness.

I'M SCARED. What if we never get back home?

"I'm afraid of heights," cried Bob.

"Bob, watch out for that bear!" yelled Joss.

"Where?" said Bob. "Where is the bear???"

"There's no bear. But now you're more afraid of bears than heights," said Joss.

"Thanks, I think."

ELEVATION: 2484 FT.
From up here, you can almost see forever.
Forever seems very far away.

Bob had an idea.

bzzz

SCRATCH
SCRATCH

Joss, climb up that tree
to see where we are.

Can you see anything?

Yes, a bear
standing next
to you.

IT'S CLIMBING UP! IT'S GOING TO EAT US!

AHHHHHHH!

This way.